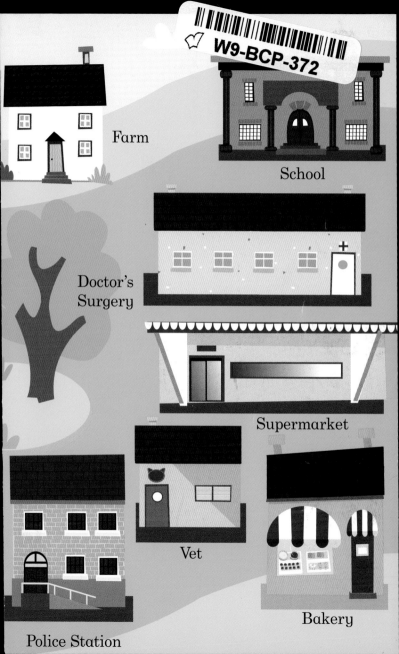

Farm

School

Doctor's Surgery

Supermarket

Vet

Bakery

Police Station

A catalogue record for this book is available from the British Library
Published by Ladybird Books Ltd
80 Strand London WC2R ORL
A Penguin Company

1 3 5 7 9 10 8 6 4 2

© LADYBIRD BOOKS MMIX

ISBN: 978-1-40930-291-9

Printed in China

Just the Job
Violet the Vet

by Mandy Ross
illustrated by Paul Nicholls

Violet the vet drove to work as usual in her blue vet van. When she arrived at the surgery, there was already a noisy queue waiting.

"What a lot of poorly pets this morning!" said Violet.

"Barker's very quiet," said
Mrs Dogsberry. "He's lost
his bark."
Violet checked Barker over.
She gave Mrs Dogsberry
some doggy tablets to put in
Barker's dinner.
"Don't worry, he'll soon be
barking again,"
she said.

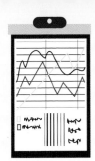
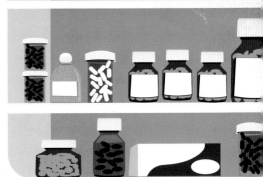

9

"Peg fell from a branch
and hurt her leg,"
said Frank the farmer.
Violet checked Peg over.
She bandaged her poorly leg.
"Don't worry, Peg will soon be
climbing trees again," she said.

"My mouse isn't moving at all," said Ben the builder. "I think she's..."
EEEK! Suddenly, the mouse leapt out of his hands.
"Hmmm," said Violet. "That mouse looks fine to me!"

13

At last, Violet had
helped all the poorly pets.
"Time to go to Frank
the farmer's," she said.
"Daisy the cow hasn't been
eating her food."
But when Violet arrived
at the farm...

15

"Daisy's gone!" said Frank the farmer, in a flap. "She was in the field earlier. She must have got out through a gap in the fence!"

"Don't worry, Frank," said Violet. "We'll find her. Now where would a runaway cow want to go?"

While Frank mended the fence, Violet looked outside the field. She noticed some hoof-prints along the lane. Violet followed the hoof-prints, until...

"Shoo! Shoo!" she heard someone shouting. It was Doris the doctor.

"Oh no!" cried Violet. There was Daisy, happily munching the flowers in front of the surgery.

Violet made a sign to Doris
to be quiet. Then she crept
up quietly behind Daisy and
slipped a rope around the
cow's neck.

"Moooooo!" mooed Daisy.

"Well, Daisy," whispered
Violet. "You seem to be
eating again."

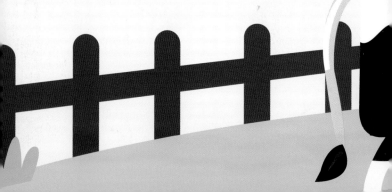

Doris the doctor and the patients waved as Violet led Daisy away from the surgery. "Everyone, please be careful to not step under Daisy's hooves," said Doris.
And no one did.

Back at the farm,
Violet checked Daisy
over. "Daisy is a very
healthy cow," she said.
"Maybe she just needs
some more flowers, as
a treat, now and then."
"Moooooo!" nodded Daisy.

Frank gave Violet a fat
round cheese, made from
Daisy's milk.

"Thank you, Violet the vet,"
he said. "We'll make sure
Daisy has plenty of flowers
to eat from now on!"

29

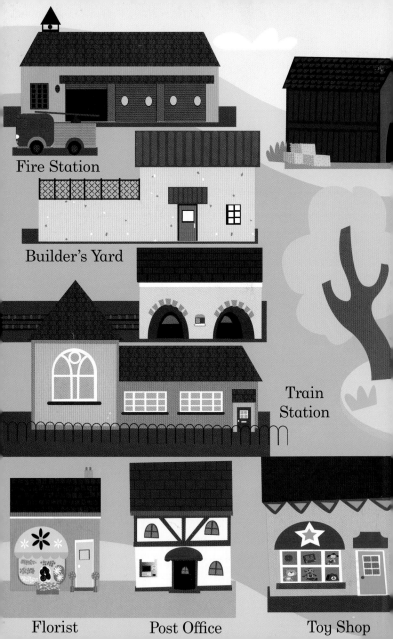

Fire Station

Builder's Yard

Train
Station

Florist

Post Office

Toy Shop